Seventy-Nine Dreams

Seventy-Nine Dreams

John Crowley

Ninepin Press
Easthampton, MA

This is a work of fiction. All characters and events portrayed in this book are either fictitious or used fictitiously.

Seventy-Nine Dreams copyright © 2024 by John Crowley.
All rights reserved.

Ninepin Press
75 Clark Street
Easthampton, MA 01027
ninepinpress.com
info@ninepinpress.com

ISBN 978-0-9964220-7-9 (paperback)
ISBN 978-0-9964220-8-6 (ebook)

Printed in the United States on 100% recycled paper. Cover art: *Trompe-l'œil à la gravure de Sarrabat* (detail) by Jean Valette-Penot.

This book is one of four volumes comprising
John Crowley's Conway Miscellany.

Kafka-esque

In the period from early 2009 to sometime late in 2010 I had a number of often lengthy and sometimes highly weird dreams that I remembered in detail on waking. I, or my brain, lately seems to have lost much of the knack of remembering dreams in this detail and completeness. While the big harvest was going on I wrote down the dreams as fully as I could, and continued less thoroughly up to 2012.

Having nothing else to do with this record, I have decided to publish what I wrote, in dated chunks that may be long or short. Some of the dates given are inexact, or wrong, but that hardly affects the reading, if anyone actually does read them. The dreams are also available to writers in need of material, who may, upon application to the author and dreamer, and with the payment of a small fee, make use of them in their own work.

March 13, 2009

L and I are lying in bed. Awakened by a door opening downstairs. I go down in the dark to find a tall man coming up, and recognize him as someone who regularly comes to take L to work somewhere. He is way too early; yet here he is, stricken. He asks if we've heard the news, the terrible thing about Holland. Suddenly I realize that I know about a dreadful, stupid, international crisis. Has Holland been bombed? I ask, and awake before I get an answer.

March 16

My yard abutted a property taken over by a sort of Orthodox Jewish group, mostly young men. They were burning brush on their property, and I had some I'd like to burn too, but I wasn't sure they'd let me burn my nonkosher brush in their fire. I brought some over, but the young men themselves weren't sure. A dispute developed about whether a nonconscious being, e.g., a robot, could commit nonkosher or forbidden acts.

March 28

In a large crowd walking through woods on their way from one meeting place to another. We passed over a border without my knowing, and I had no passport to get back—only a damp and illegible ID card. Then at an airline desk asking my daughter if she had *her* passport. Trouble, flights canceled and delayed. Then I am driving with my agent Ralph through a Midwestern city at evening—his kindly, courtly Chinese dream-assistant telling me that the bill for the car, which L had rented, would be $800.

March 29

No memory of the part where I lost something or suffered some setback—but then out on dark city streets. Saw a young, tough girl driving a crazy three-wheeled motorcycle—admired her toughness and skill. But she was going too fast on the potholed road, wouldn't stop, finally lost control and was flung out onto the street. I was following—in a car now—and stopped and got out. People had gathered—among them her boyfriend, it seemed, grief-crazed—he was picking her up to carry her to a hospital—actually piggyback, her head lolling. I yelled after him to stop, he wouldn't, I ran to my car to follow him but the car was gone. I'd left the key in it. Stolen, in the one minute since I abandoned it.

Then somehow in a low hostel crowded with unsavory types, moneyless, without the car (which I realized belonged to my agent, as in the dream of the night before). A kindly hostel director asked for the rent—I had none—I tried to explain everything to him and began to sob terribly over all that had gone wrong: the money, the car, the thing that had happened before, whatever it was. Sobs that woke me.

April 8

Getting married. A big family, all hers, gathered in the living and dining rooms. It seemed a 1930s middle-class apartment. A relative, an older man, made a long speech. Someone next to me—I knew him but can't remember now who it was—said that I was the one who should have made that speech: questioning my commitment. The bride-to-be somewhat dim, a mousy, slight girl—my relation with her cool and not passionate. I went upstairs to the bathroom and searched my feelings—did I really want to do this? Wasn't there some horror or reluctance in me? And no, there wasn't. I was happy about it, and about her, even if I hardly knew her.

I woke then, and slept again, and the dream continued. I was talking with her—she less mousy and diminished now. I felt I could look at this face a long time. She was telling me about a bad boring time in her life when the only interesting thing that kept her going was listening to William F. Buckley on the radio. I was a little alarmed at that and hoped she was listening to Buckley only because she found him outrageous and funny—but I didn't know her well enough to be sure.

April 24

Turning into my driveway I felt I had driven over something but couldn't be sure. I got out and looked, and saw a crow had got entangled under there. It came out, shaken and hurt but not badly. I tried to urge it to go into the garage, where I would care for it and nurse it back to health. I was secretly delighted at this chance. The crow had meanwhile grown considerably larger, buzzard-sized. I did get it to go into the garage, and we began a conversation about the feasibility of my plan. The crow was doubtful. By now it had transformed into a young girl with black hair, while remaining a crow. Sure, I said, we'll have you back to hunting in no time. Ugh, she said, I hate hunting.

May 7

Walking through a series of public rooms, looking in on a string quartet—no, a small vocal group—practicing. I passed a room where chairs and tables were arranged so people could witness something at one table, where my friend Larry (who in actuality had died a few weeks before) and his first wife sat, looking just as they had in 1963, he in a tie and blazer. I felt shy about joining him or speaking to them; there was something wrong about this. But I did, and they were glad to see me at first; we chatted about how this return of the past could be possible. Then Larry start to slump over onto me in some kind of painless agony, distorting him, slack-jawed. I knew he was dead and the illusion was over, and I woke up crying aloud.

Another, later: A complicated dark city dream, driving and parking, having a long cell-phone conversation with a producer I was writing with, on a film about cars (the Shelby Ford Cobra was mentioned), who was displeased and complaining.

And just now remembering a long-ago dream—don't know from when—about an elaborate and ancient parking garage, trying to find my car. So dreams *don't* vanish away—they remain in waiting.

May 15

Watching a TV documentary about a rural community practicing their annual ritual of peeling potatoes. Long table set up outdoors, people facing one another on each side with peelers in their hands. Rich saturated color photography, joyous conversation, maybe even love affairs starting (by now I was *in* the doc, not watching it). Moving through a kitchen space with a cloth bag that had held my potatoes; someone washing things in a deep soapy tub. Did I want to wash my bag? No—there was only a little earth in the bottom.

Sleep, and wake—and now in a big city. Agreeing with someone like John Goodman that we should commandeer a trolley car to get where we were going. I look back to see him taking off in the trolley without me, and I chase madly after it on foot but have time to notice how nice the neighborhood is, town houses and brick sidewalks and the cute trolley line. I take a bus, hoping to intersect with the trolley. At first packed, then transformed to a dark long-distance bus; the only passenger is my longtime friend Lance, in a discussion with Paul Park about literary fame. Lance was smoking voluptuously, his head wreathed in smoke.

May 22

In a large messy country house owned by a rich businessperson, and I need to get back to the city. The owner's young male assistants assuring me that I could get a ride in his limo back to the city when he left. But it had begun to snow. Then the millionaire himself appeared—he went about tidying up the mess his assistants had left—soda bottles, etc.—tolerant of them but also critical or contemptuous. Assured me he'd get me home.

Woke, and then found myself in another huge space, talking with women—producers who were working out a rehearsal, how they were going to get us all to the city. Just then I remembered that this was the day I was to go into outer space. I wondered if the space team had called me at home and I wasn't there—I didn't even know where I was supposed to report. Woke up laughing.

June 14

Meeting M. She supposedly was older than when I last saw her, but not in this dream. Long exchange with her, about how she was the one I loved and suffered most for. How we had not kept together. I told her that the reason was she'd never really believed I loved her. That was false—she knew I loved her inordinately; the problem was she didn't love me.

June 16

In bed with an aged king (played by an aged Peter O'Toole; it seemed a movie and not a play). He was decaying—skin pocked and loathsome—and needed to have sex with me in order to restore his own youth. *Your perfect white skin*, he said—me seeming to be a youth in the dream. Some feeling of disgust and possible pain—anal intercourse—but not unwilling to try to help. An alchemical dream, in effect. The decaying king resembled not only Peter O'Toole but, even more, a Berkeley College fellow I'd encountered the week before in the streets of New Haven.

June 26

At an outdoor café with friends—drawn away by a threatening man of a kind I encounter in dreams—sadist or power mad, fiery eyed and irrational. He has a grip on me and takes me down the block a ways and lays out his reasons for needing to kill me—I forget what those were. I try to gently counter his madness and allay his cold rage. No luck. He demands I keep still and come with him quietly. I see a chance to signal one of my friends at the café table, but somebody else, whom I don't know, thinks the signal is for him, and he waves in a friendly fashion. But now I've given away my cry-for-help signal. Things looking very bad for me as I wake.

July 11

Endless. In a huge dark crowded train station or transportation hub. L and I going to New Hampshire, but I don't have the right papers—I have my passport but it needs to be renewed. I go to find an office where this can be done. Small dim shabby space, people milling around in old clothes, or with bundles on benches, like a welfare office. An inner office where a thin Chinese woman has brought a bag of groceries for a co-worker. Long wait. Another woman—most of the agents and officials are women—draws a plastic curtain between our space and the offices.

August 9

I was a younger man—poor—single—in the city. I needed a car, and found a large ancient rusted and battered van for sale very cheap. It even had a toilet in the back. I knew my parents would find this purchase odd, but I thought it was a great deal (maybe it was free). A couple of young women near me were also enjoying it.

Then, out with it on the streets of a big sunlit city. The van became a small bus, and I'd got a job as a freelance bus driver (my bus was the van, still shabby and rusted). I picked up people at corners, got stuck in various ways and places, people called out in annoyance or gave advice. I didn't know the city, or at least this part of it. At last stopped and let out my disgusted passengers. One who'd been kind, a young tourist, stayed with me. He and two friends (one in a black velvet cutaway coat) were out to see religious shrines connected to their faith. "If I could find the Shrine of Our Lady of Loreto," I said, "I could get oriented, and know where I should take you." But—they said—that's far away, up on the top of a hill. Did I mean *that* shrine? (Pointing to a sort of Moorish-looking building.) "No," I said, "that's Temple Immanuel."

But we were now standing in front of a small white marble building—shrine to some lay saint-like figure—and I thought this was maybe the place I had meant to reach. The sweet young Christian tourists and I went in. A person who welcomed us there—old, with an affect like Morgan Freeman—told me I wasn't done with bus-driving. From an ancient printer in a dark office he produced a paper—my route! Now I'll know where to go, what turns to take on what streets. I told the Christian (his friends were gone) that I am very bad at directions—he said he'd guide me (!). We set out. I thought maybe I could become just a gypsy bus and keep all the fares, but decided that would be wrong, and probably I'd be caught at it anyway.

* *This dream—the failure, the spiritual guide, the shrine, the wise keeper of the shrine, the task given me, the guide remaining by my side, the temptation to backslide—was so like myth that I could sense its hieratic force even asleep, though only awake could I grasp it.*

August 30

L was getting married to a sort of ordinary man named Hubert or Herbert—nice enough, but she wasn't in love with him. Did want a big wedding, after all these years, which he could supply. I gave advice. Sometimes we seemed to have the history we have and sometimes not—dream paradox. L seemed reconciled but at the same time deeply troubled and shaky and near tears.

September, no date:

L and I were servants of Lord Byron. Working in a great shabby kitchen. No suggestion of a past era. Byron was off on a journey. We quibbled about something in the kitchen. Then I took a leftover pizza we thought Byron might want on his return and went to put it in a refrigerator in an adjoining room, also huge, dirty, and dark. The refrigerator, apparently antique or period—it was a large box surmounted by a huge black stove, glowing red with heat, which made the box cold. Or maybe it was to reheat the pizza?

September, no date:

I was living in an apartment with a Latino family, a middle-aged man and children. I saw smoke rising from the floor beneath the window curtain, or between the curtain and the window. We all have to escape. More smoke in another room. I go into a bedroom where I know the ill and senile grandma is. I explain to her ("Nana") that we have to go, and I pick her up, tiny, just skin and bones.

The strange thing was that all this seemed to be happening in a play or movie, and I knew what to say, what would happen, and would recognize it when it did—the smoke, the reactions of the people, my own speech and actions, coming as on cue, or as though rehearsed and familiar.

October 4

Walking in Berlin in the 1930s. A little afraid of being recognized as not belonging there, and not belonging *then* either. I'm wearing a wool suit and a heavy wool overcoat. A door leads to a bar that announces it's the oldest in the city, or very historic anyway. Pushing through, I find myself still on the street—it's a sidewalk sort of affair despite the wall and the door. A patron is passed out head down on the bar. I have no money—I ask the cashier where I can go to change money. Right here, she says. She changes my American bills to German currency. I can order a beer without speaking German—just point to one of the enormous beer-pulls.

Same night: I brought food to a cat kept in an enclosure. It began to burrow rapidly down through a hole in a corner of the enclosure. Someone next to me said, *He just wants to see San Marco one more time!* The cat then worked his way backwards up through the dirt to appear again—his tunnel had somehow fallen in and he could go no farther. Intense feeling of claustrophobia on awaking.

October 6

Walking through a suburban neighborhood along the backyards. Several swimming pools. Because of climate change the water and the pools had changed to a milky white. In each pool was an alligator. I went to my own backyard, glad I didn't have a pool, but when I reached it I could see that in the yard were several large alligators. Skirted them carefully, feeling that we will all have to be very careful from now on.

October, no date:

Met a young couple, boy and girl, very attractive, slight; boy with a sort of Caesar haircut, lightly orange skin, his hair too. His name was Victor. It became clear they wanted to have sex with me. So pleasant and cool and cheerful. I was thrilled. We walked the streets of the usual dark city, but somewhere the girl was separated from us, and I was sorry. Victor said no, she has something to do, she'll meet us later at my place. We started that way. Very grateful that I could get to have sex with this beautiful (now shirtless) slight, lithe person. Awoke.

December 18

In a shabby American rural environment—can't recall what led up to it, but I was in a sort of shed, where there was a long wooden box or trough filled with dead leaves. I don't know how I got the idea to begin wading in this box, kicking up the leaves. This uncovered various items buried in them, some of them valuable. A woman talking to me thought this was a waste of time when I had a plane to catch, but I kept at it. Turned up money, a few ones and fives, and sort of tag-sale items, a creepy fake-Chinese decorative teapot, some silverware—save it for my daughters?— and a wooden spoon like that one of L's that broke. I knew with increasing certainty that this enterprise wasn't worth it.

Finally traveling with the woman, or another woman, in a big car through the compound where this shed and other buildings were. Big blue sky, flat agricultural area. "This is Mennonite country," she said. "Places like this have a deep emotional meaning for those who live here all their lives." I said I understood very well. She dropped me off at another building. Reaching in my back pocket I found my wallet gone—only a loose pack of credit cards. What happened then to all that money that I found? I tried to believe it was safe but began to be overwhelmed by a dreadful sense that I'd made wrong choices, missed my plane, everything was going very badly, I was a fool and trapped. Awoke.

December 19

Nightmare of a common kind I have: In a realistic environment something impossible happens, proof that occult powers are present and acting in the world. In this one, I'm standing by the door of the back hall when one of my old rubber Wellingtons begins flopping horribly all on its own across the floor. As often in these dreams I am afraid but try to stand up to the things—stamp on the squirming boot—but then the closet door opened and empty coats and dresses began coming forth and reaching for me. L woke me up screaming.

December 20

With various members of my family in the offices of an old and respected *parfumier*—his name was Fischer but the perfume company had a different name—not a brand in the waking world. He began showing me small samples of his most famous perfumes. I said I wasn't good at perfumes, though I remember vividly some from my youth that still have a powerful impact when I encounter them.

It appeared that this conversation with Fischer was a job interview, which was not going to go well since I know nothing about the perfume business, and also because I was in my bathrobe. My mother—who'd got me the interview and was looking on hopefully—began kidding with another interviewee, who couldn't answer even one question: State the name of another famed perfume company, as shown in an ad in a glossy magazine: Frieda K… "Oh, come on," we all said. "Frieda Kahlo!"

December 21

Brief one: driving on a flat landscape and seeing in the sky huge numbers of large white balloons very high up, and more soaring upward from the ground—they began to form geometrical shapes which vanished as soon as formed—like kaleidoscope patterns. It became clear that it was an art show, like fireworks made of air. I could guess at the physics that caused the balloons to come together and then burst, thus seeming to vanish. Thrilling but vertiginous.

December 22

Teaching a fiction-writing class—trying to get students to identify the central problems that make one piece of fiction different from another. We take a break and everyone goes out—we are in large, dark-windowed ground-floor space—and I decide to go take a bunch of books out of the library and read the first sentences to the class to make the distinctions clear. Two students—a male and a female—volunteer to help, and we go to the library, a huge cavernous building like a deserted Gilded Age mansion, and of course can't find the stacks. Up and then down to basement levels, crowded now with people and brightly lit like a mall or airport shopping area, and I know I'll never get those books or find my class again in time.

December 23

With Paul Park on some kind of rooftop terrace—an art or literary event there involving us reading or speaking or both. A nice buffet. It appears the events are to be video-recorded, so I take the opportunity while lunch is on to drive home and change clothes. As in the dream above, and in so many like it, this plan takes longer than I expect: every piece of clothing is wrong or dirty or made of camo (!). Eventually I decide on a sort of hospital undershirt with snaps. It buttons between the legs like a child's onesie, but no matter. However, this garment transmutes the surroundings into a hospital, and a nurse and a child patient appear, watching me, wondering what I'm up to, which I try to explain. The hospital, an ancient one, is high ceilinged, an old-time bare ward, white iron bedsteads.

December 26

Dream of riding in a car with Tom Disch. He was driving, and we were having a dispute or contention about some matter. He tried to call someone he knew for corroboration, on an elaborate car phone that included a radio and big headphones. Feeling at one moment that I should express love for him in some way, because he was in fact dead, or would soon be dead, and I wouldn't otherwise get the chance. I took his shoulder in a grip. Finally the phone machinery fragmented away to the point that he was gone and I was alone in a house. At the direction of someone (a family member?) I was hanging up the key to the car-phone system in a special cabinet filled with saved things and other keys.

December 28

In a mall or public space with the kids, who were young, as they often are in these dreams, and passing a sort of pitchman dressed as a space traveler, doing a pseudo-informative lecture on something—actually a pitch for a product, using a high-tech display/video. I heard him behind me saying something about homosexuals. "Tests have shown that on average they are X percent less intelligent than others." I marched back and confronted him, showing his misuse of statistics. It appeared then that the pitchman was not just dressed as a spaceman; he was in fact William Shatner, down on his luck (and having lost a lot of weight). Somewhat sheepish about his pitch, which he was only doing for the money.

Same night: In a large meeting around a circular table—huge—crowded with people, plus many young students sitting on the floor. The meeting is all about my books. Embarrassing wish fulfillment? Regardless, critical remarks are made. My sister Jo across the table offered interesting and insightful arguments about some aspects of a book of mine, but a standard academic person started off on a different topic. Recommended Jo's insight over the academic's ramble but was ignored. Again noted that it should be paid attention to, until L. kicked me under the table, *Shut up.*

January 12, 2010

I was invited to a street-theater or public-festival production of a Shakespeare play. Dark city where preparations and rehearsals were going on. In one space as small as a shrine or a bank's ATM area, a father or maybe the director was rehearsing two young girls in a famous scene where they approach the picture of their dead mother, speaking about it and her in Shakespearean images I of course can't remember. I commented to others who stood around that it was wonderful how the director/producer had substituted common modern nouns for those of the Elizabethans, so that the play could be more contemporary. I was speaking now at a sidewalk café to other participants—I was playing, and somehow also being, a courtier or best-friend figure. Rehearsals were to begin for a scene we were to be in, and I didn't know my lines—couldn't even imagine them—and began searching fruitlessly through a thick script for the pages I needed.

January 19

Sandy McClatchy [Yale professor and colleague] came to my house. He paid the place a compliment on entering (he's never been here), and well he might. The house was not my actual house but an immense Victorian pile, grand circular staircase, ceilings twenty feet high, excessive furniture, all dark gleaming wood. Awoke, laughed, slept again, and the dream continued—Sandy and I in the library of this place at work preparing a script for a sort of masque or old interlude for a new performance. Parts had to be copied out from a stack of ancient printed copies full of obscuring baroque decoration.

February 2

Much dreaming lately but mostly scraps and ends:

—I remember sitting with a Buddhist monk in a school lunchroom who told me that the two components of matter are earth and smoke.

—A town meeting where I was challenged by an official to prove my address, having to go through first my wallet and then the usual multiplying pile of miscellaneous papers for some bill with my address on it.

—Also one where I was part of a group in an experimental station of some kind—lengthy test-taking I don't remember. Mostly young people. A group of them were wandering around the strange landscape, taking the role of the first visitors to an alien planet—a sort of thought experiment—and examining the surroundings.

Then tests that had been done on my heart and body began to be transmitted to this crowded center where work was going forward. The transmission was displayed on an overhead screen, the data represented by the image of an airplane flying in—very 1950s. But the transmission caused oscilloscopes behind glass and hammer-finish registers to fibrillate and shake apart, spewing fan-fold punched paper. This was all right, I was told, it just showed my test results, but I ought to consult with my doctors.

February 11

Longest and most harrowing can't-find-my-way dream I can remember. Began with L and the girls and me on a trip. We came to a stock-car museum and theme park where visitors could drive race cars against other visitors on a track. We signed up for this—had to get in line. I couldn't figure out where we should go to get our cars; went across the track to where somebody—guide, official—was explaining things to a group of visitors in a sort of rocky glen—much like the scenery in the *Lucia di Lammermoor* production I had recently seen. Can we get in line here? Where? Do you have a car with hand controls? Oh yes, just go down that way and over there, etc. I tried to follow his instructions but was soon elsewhere—in a building, asking for help—none of it led to anywhere I needed to go, keenly aware of my lack of a sense of direction, couldn't keep the directions given to me in my head. I went into dark back halls of an old and gloomy hotel, was directed to go down to a damp, dark pissoir (a sign, "Pissoir," over the door) and take a left; I entered a pleasant restaurant full of happy people (by now I was downtown in a Midwestern city) and then a huge old factory with moving machines but no workers. Passing through I thought, *Oh, this is the kind of place where I get those images in my dreams!* Finally, catwalks or flown platforms in a train station—I could see a cart trundling toward me carrying huge suitcases and luggage, and the platforms begin sliding, moving beneath me, collapsing: great danger. Woke up.

March 4

In a small apartment bedroom with L (maybe my old place on 10th street in New York). We were arguing about some piece of writing I have agreed to do for her. This involved reworking or incorporating all the entries in a children's encyclopedia of mythology. I finally conceded; we go to bed (actually she'd been arguing her plan from bed). Dream continues with me trying to tell her something about this project, she now asleep and unable to wake—no shaking or calling does it. Then a later scene (I may have fallen asleep and then awakened) where she was now up and about, self-possessed and calmly amused while I went on about the stupid project.

March, no date:

I am in a historic house, grand, Federal, and a magician/craftsman is creating glass balls: He does this by dipping a wand in some sort of solution and then drawing upward the drop on the wand, which instead of dropping off inflates into a globe, like a glass paperweight, full of colored bits. I ask if they are actually solid. Oh yes—if they are left to harden and treated with care they are permanent. I'm given charge of one of them—now a sort of flared-rim vase—and told to carry it carefully to the basement.

No date:

A wake-up-screaming one. I was on a bed with my children, and other children too—with us was a large robot of possibly dangerous temperament—very slow moving and Golem-like, made of metal struts. He obeyed commands, but you couldn't tell how long he would; he seemed intent on messing or interfering somehow with the children, so I inveigled him into a closet by telling one of the children to go in, which tempted him to follow. The kid slipped out and I shut the door on the robot. He made his way out then and began to be menacing, getting worked up in some way. Finally I grasped him and he tumbled over, now crying out something unintelligible. I tried to calm him but it was no use. He was now crying *Bloody Paul! Bloody Paul!* and I began to understand that he had done something terrible to a child and felt the horror of it himself. He was holding *me* now in a deathly grip, I was crying out to him, his eye sockets had turned into pits of dark-red dried-blood vacuity. Then L woke me up—I'd been moaning horribly.

April, no date:

A fun one. Staying at some kind of mountain resort, I had participated with L and Bill, her research assistant, in stealing a bag of jewels. We threw them into the trunk of an old sedan that Bill was driving, possibly a rent-a-wreck, and took off into the night. We passed a cop car that seemed to set out in pursuit but might have been going after someone else; but Bill decided to lose him by turning off onto a dirt road down which we sped, then up an impossibly steep and rocky and narrow mountain road, Bill very cool at the wheel. We came to a big roadhouse—sat having drinks and swapping small talk with the patrons, though I felt a little worried about our crime.

Later: Somehow I had decided to book a room back in the earlier hotel where we had stolen the jewels, thinking there was no way I could be identified as one of the thieves—but on going into the bathroom I found that various toiletries I had abandoned in my previous room had been transferred to this room, proving they knew very well I was the same person. L showed up, and I had to conceal my fears from her.

April 6

Finding my way up a wooded bank onto a cobbled road in the night (escaping? From what?) and finding myself in a large auditorium. I sat in the balcony while a band set up on stage. I knew some of the players, and I watched the rehearsal. The seats around me filled up with others, friends or guests of the band, joking and laughing; ushers came around offering treats, drinks, cigars. I made my way from there to a daytime beach, climbed another embankment, and from there came into a small seaside town, where I became entangled with a Chinese laundry (I was in the past now) whose owner thought I was stealing laundry or doing some other mischief, and he locked me in the building, whose walls were a beautiful blue—old painted wood doors with ancient locks. I was trying to get out when the laundryman's twin brother caught me. I tried to explain. He and his brother were both tall handsome men with thick long black hair. The dream ended with me telling the twin that he and his brother would do well in the movies.

May 8

At Bill Cosby's enormous house (in waking life L and I had driven by there the day before, Cosby a longtime homeowner in our town). In the dream I'm lying next to him on pillows in a lounge. I asked why he didn't act any more—he could play a different kind of role now. The lounge became a bed we were both lying in. He seemed old, bored, sad. Someone put a sandwich next to me. I thanked Bill for ordering it.

Then: walking in New Haven with some papers that Bill had asked me to look over. They became a manuscript, or rather a typescript, pages heavily corrected, that John Updike had asked my opinion on. I hadn't responded, and now felt guilty and tried to assess the work, but of course I was unable to read it. Then I realized or remembered: Updike's dead. I have no reason to respond, I waited too long and now my response can mean nothing to him.

* *This dream came long before the revelations that would lead to Cosby's arrest and conviction.*

May 13

A long, anxious dream. I was in a huge mansion or country house—my daughters had been invited there to be part of an event celebrating something, or to attend classes there—anyway they didn't want to (as usual they were about twelve, Z in her braces). They had escaped from the group and were hiding out in a room in the mansion, where they intended to hole up. There would be consequences if they were discovered there. H thought it was a great secret place where they'd never be found, but I pointed out that the room had a wide window looking out onto the grounds. They were unconcerned. How would they spend their time, hidden away? The sounds from the room would draw attention.

Somehow then I was alone in the room—they'd gone exploring—I was very nervous—I tried to write them a note to tell them I had to go or I'd be caught—of course I couldn't write—useless pen, tiny scraps of paper dense with print. I heard a group coming with a teacher or leader—ah! I remember now, it was an older woman, imperious, in whose house we were—and I was again afraid of being caught there where I didn't belong, as the door now stood wide open. Then suddenly H and Z snuck in.

They'd been following the group and now dodged away. Cheerful and proud of themselves for their ruse. I wanted them to understand their peril, but I could take no action.

August 16

Tonight a wonderful falling-in-love dream charged with that blissful ecstatic mingling of souls in delight that's rare and impossible in such purity in waking life. I can't remember many details—my memory of any dream that I *do* remember is impaired because I can rarely remember what was *said*—only pictures of the events and the consequent feelings. She was Latina, and we met in Florida. Instant (of course) ease and sweetness and possibility. We were rooming with others and couldn't find privacy—once snatching a moment when we could, pants down quick, but too late, someone's coming. I began to think of abandoning my life up north (where I had a wife or woman, though not L) and just living on here in Florida—but would I like a world of no autumns and winters? I didn't care, I just wanted her.

Then we were not in the South but in Brattleboro, she a stranger there and surprised it was so flat. I explained that it was an odd geological formation that made for this particular region. We went into a sort of park near a huge church—a cathedral—I thinking I must know what church this is but unable to remember—then sitting with her in a pew, overwhelmed with a sense of delight and wonder at my good fortune and the return, however briefly, of this superb feeling—laughed aloud—she asked me why—I woke.

August 25

Walking from one venue to another of some sort of literary conference in the rain, talking with a famous leonine literary person about a magazine where a piece of mine was appearing. Couldn't remember the name. "The project of a rich man who can do as he likes," I said and then realized I shouldn't have said that and it wasn't true. Then I recalled the name of the elderly man, and the name of the journal—*Lapham's Quarterly* [where a piece of mine would appear in waking life]. We went on to where a symposium of some kind would be held, in fact a schoolroom where the chairs and desks were child sized. I was to read a piece asked for by the leonine gent, and I didn't have it—but found I could produce a carbon copy at least—though when I looked at the onionskin sheets I saw that they had been typed over some business letters. Distress and anxiety.

August 31

Two brief ones: I was in my family circle, or a combination of my family and my birth family—my mother, my father, who was complaining that while we were happy to get together with my mother alone, when it was *he* who was alone we didn't want to gather and be with him. We poo-poohed this but knew it was true. *[It's impossible for me, when awake, to think of my father making a self-pitying complaint like this.]* I got away from him and went to my room and tried to assemble a computer from parts— one had a white cord coming out from it that had actually been scissored off.

Then reading a text of Harold Bloom's, in which he was responding to criticisms of his style as mandarin and unfeeling (!). As the text went on, it became expressive and fragmented— ". . . memory of home and wife . . . warm feelings as I reach the end of this sentence . . ."—and I woke.

November 4

Very long and multipart dream while spooning with L on a cold night—began as a car ride with the family—passing through a festive city—a huge narrow tower like one of the towers of Sagrada Familia in Barcelona but made of something translucent—amazing. The city then became a funfair where we wandered—H was complaining that her writing teacher refused to let her do the story she wanted because it wasn't complete—L not very sympathetic, and tears came to H's eyes as they can do—I got very angry at the stupid teacher who had no idea how to teach writing or encourage students. L and I came to a coffee shop where I sat at a counter with my friend David Gates, who gave me a piece of criticism or advice that I forget. He went away, leaving behind a collection of mystery magazines containing his own work, and an elaborate typewriter/computer combo.

L and I walked away from this place and out to the road through to woods where we saw a small black sports car rushing our way. It went past us at high speed, seemed to lose control, swerving and banging the guardrail and then smashing into some trees at a driveway—flipping and torn in pieces. We rushed to help, and when we got there people from the house were already pulling at the wreckage to get the driver out. It seemed then that the car had held several people, a whole family and several kids ages ten or eleven in the crushed back of the car—which had become more like a minivan—and we expected to find them horrified and traumatized by their father's mangled corpse, but no such vision was shown them or me; it was assumed they'd had a bad experience, and the people in the house (a different house now, more upscale) tried to entertain them at a picnic or barbecue that had been underway when the accident occurred. I remember two girls of the stricken family talking about dresses.

It was now night. A cat, which had apparently also been in the car, came around me to be fed or comforted—traumatized also—and as a kindly Burl Ives type in a lawn chair looked on approvingly, I let the cat curl up in my lap.

December, no date

Last night, a long and circumstantial one. It starts with me living in a sort of communal house overseen by a commanding but generous older man (like several dreams in this form) with young men around. I wandered, searching—went into a bedroom that had windows onto a game room where some of the residents were engaging in horseplay and ping-pong. I found a pornography book. The boss or owner or leader came in. "I see you have discovered my bedroom," he said—at which I was embarrassed—I hadn't known this—but he was amused and tolerant.

Then there's a gap—I don't remember leaving this place—only setting out on an urgent trip someplace. I was in an elevator carrying me down into an old and shabby interurban underground train system, fully furnished with scarred walls and old technology as usual, and I was thinking how to account to L for the days I had spent in that previous environment. I realized: Oh, I don't have to account for it, it was after all a dream and took up no real time at all.

January 14, 2010

> *Lots of rich dreaming recently, along with periods of no memory or slipping memories. I have to write down the ones I remember or they erode quickly.*

Last night—seeing Lynda *[a former friend]* with some man at a table in a restaurant—amazed and a little horrified. My Dream Manager tried to alter her a little to reflect her real age, but in the dream she was young. Then she and I got together, and already I've forgotten what was said, but as the dream progressed it seemed she wanted my help in writing a screenplay—and now we were in the dark, outdoors (the beach?) comparing various versions on white tablet computers. Then I was induced (by her, maybe, though she then disappeared) to go to a hotel, which consisted of a series of tiny rooms done in a fussy Victorian style. I wandered, needing to get out—I was shown to a tall window, which was opened for me. I had to climb up and over the sill, and saw that it was a steep drop to the street, but of course I accepted all this and jumped down, to where a friendly couple (he with a drink in his hand) greeted me encouragingly. Their horrid fanged dog, though, took a dash at me and ripped my pants leg with his teeth. I started to look for where Lynda had gone, now cognizant of how young she'd looked—*If I'm 77, she'd be 67!* And thereupon I began a helpless search for where I'd parked my car.

January 20

Against my will I had got a job working for a slumlord in New York City, going around to his buildings and checking in with the supers about some matter. I was carrying a list of the addresses I was to go to. At some of these decaying buildings no one answered the bell, and I had to find a pay phone to call. Cursed myself for having forgotten my cellphone (though I was obviously in a world before the cellphone was invented). At one building I couldn't enter—it was a restaurant, not yet open—at last the chef let me in—a tiny place—we chatted—then my errand was forgotten—I sat at a table for a meal, the tables tiny and arranged like old-fashioned school desks. Flirted mildly with a young woman diner at the next table.

January 28

The dream began as a documentary about an American who had gone to a South American country and adopted local customs and way of life. He'd become a purveyor of a special kind of smoked or broiled beef, which he had to carry to local shops. He had a white horse (which soon wasn't seen any more), and the man in one scene had to cross a jungle pool or lagoon, pushing his wares before him on a little raft as he walked in water up to his chest. At about this point the guy became myself; I was dealing with a shop owner—it was like a butcher shop, except that it sold only these cooked meats. He was also an American who had adopted this life. He set me to slicing up the meat, which came in huge slabs like briskets. It looked delicious. I was given a sharp knife, but I was inexperienced with it somehow, and the shop owner took me to task for cutting the pieces too small. He let me know that locals liked big slices, not small, and if I didn't cut them properly, my meats would be held in contempt. I would be revealed as a know-nothing outsider.

As I labored, the dream changed, and I was more customer than purveyor, the shop now larger and more like a restaurant. L and the girls arrived—H in a dress, ordering a special kind of beer with great exactness, in Spanish. They had been staying in a nearby city and had come out for the day on an expedition.

February 4

While L was out of town, I bought a house for us—we had been looking for a new place to live and this one seemed wonderful and cheap—a big old rambling farmhouse, shabby but lovable—small outbuildings connected to the big house in New England style. I sat at a table in the garden (the long-ago kitchen garden) and counted the units—13! I was sure this place was a steal at $112,000, but I felt that L wouldn't be happy at my precipitate action. Many people around now, the sellers of the house and friends of mine. Drops of rain started to fall and we all went back inside—I stood on the front porch, which would need work—the rain grew very heavy—I went inside and found that the ceiling was leaking badly—rivulets coursing down over a set of rather depressing red plastic stuffed furniture. The walls now appearing dark and splotched with wetness. I tried to tell myself that even if upgrading cost a hundred thou it would be worth it. Tried to call L to tell her what I'd decided to do, and somehow the phone let me in on a conversation she was having with a neighbor, someone she'd known in the film business before—and she couldn't hear me at all. Ended the call in distress and anxiety.

February 15

In a hospital office or examination room with L and the kids, aged five or six. Z was to undergo some sort of treatment, and to prepare for this I had to submit an affidavit that would be entered into a large machine and examined to see if my emotional commitment to the procedure was high enough. I was having trouble understanding or assenting to this, and my sample was determined to be insufficiently empathetic. The on-call nurse was kindly but impatient with my inability to produce the right stuff. Meanwhile the girls had been playing, copying cartoons out the *New Yorker* with amazing skill. L was beginning the medical process, putting a cloth mask over Z's head and gauze strips over the eyeholes—Z with that strange, awesome patience with which she used to put up with such things when she really was five. At last L went to a sort of electric typewriter, and—tears in her eyes—typed something that should be sufficient to pass the test (*she* was certainly showing empathy). The writing was in a large bold font, a couple of lines I could read. *Oh all right fine, this will do*—I was now impatient, and angry with her for having done this when I couldn't, and for giving in to them.

Another nurse came in to collect the statement, and I looked down at the papers I held, and it wasn't among them! But that's *absurd*, I *just had it*—I looked on the floor, crawled under the desk, profoundly exasperated—and then I began to realize the only explanation for the disappearance of the statement: *This is all a dream!* I looked around the very solid and actual office, the walls, the windows, desks, machines—but *yes, dammit, it's a dream!* I was furious with triumph, and to prove I was right I lifted myself off the floor and into the air. At which point L shook me awake—I'd been yelling aloud in a horror-stricken nightmare voice, and I couldn't convince her it hadn't actually been a bad dream.

February 19

In an apartment with L and I couldn't sleep. A large, gray, shabby multilevel housing complex. I got up at last and went out of the room and down into an empty or abandoned apartment below. As I explored this place, I was somehow made aware of a ghostly presence in the doorway—a shadow on the half-open door. Thinking that whatever or whoever it was might not want me here, I began trying to explain that I was just wandering lost—my words thick in my throat—obviously I was on the point of waking in terror—but I fell again into deeper sleep and began my explanation again—at which point the spooky figure resolved itself into a young woman, short dark hair. She and I began talking and perhaps went to her apartment on the ground floor of the complex, a storefront. She was like a student—but I was a young person too, in the dreamworld, and something might have come of it, but others began to arrive and we all chatted together. Then I realized how late it must be and how long I'd been away from L. So I said goodnight—they were friendly, except for one male who might have been her boyfriend, who glared somewhat at me, but I made him shake my hand—come on, I'm no threat.

I went back upstairs and found my sister Kathy in a bedroom, lying on a mattress on the floor with someone, child or partner, playing a game with strange counters, and I asked her what time it was. Eleven o'clock. In the *morning*!? How would I account for all those hours to L? Woke up.

No dates:

A long spell of only tale-ends [*sic*] and moments. Last night a dream of having two girlfriends, one tall and large, the other small and plump. I could retain both somehow, but then seeing them together I realized they'd be forever fighting over me for the top slot [!].

On a bus, insisting that the driver make a special stop for me and a companion, but with the necessity of exiting out the window, because the stop was unscheduled, and dropping to the ground—the window absurdly small and the ground dangerously far away. And what about my luggage?

One about the end of the world—atomic war, and more—but all I remember is somber nighttime architecture of blank cement walls and a view off into the night and the coast far away, where a line of bombs was going off silently. Can't remember the man who stood beside me there—someone I know well.

One I remember in detail was about working for Michael Jackson. He didn't much resemble the actual Michael Jackson except for being insulated and self-indulgent. Living in a townhouse in New York crowded with hangers-on. He had rewritten a script of mine, many times in fact, and his drafts were piled before me, including his latest, twice the length of the others, and I was to read them all and extract the best of each. I refused—Michael, I'm not going to read all this, it's useless! We negotiated how the job might be done. Then we were in a small gondola-like boat going down the Hudson River, and he was telling me about his poetry—which he wrote, he said, because it gave him a sense of structure and restraint, unlike the scripts. I was to read the poetry too. I made it clear that I really didn't want to, but he began to exhibit signs of neurotic fragility, and the last part of the dream was returning with him to the townhouse at night and reassuring him, an arm around him, that I'd do what he wanted, he wasn't to worry.

June 8

In a large apartment, like a loft, with large windows and several doors, I met Lori A. Supposedly now older but actually looking as she did thirty years ago, though more mature in attitude. We decide to have sex—finally—for reasons I can't remember. She has to go away and make some arrangements before this happens. Alone in the apartment, I go into rooms and alcoves, shutting doors left open, so that we can have privacy. Then as I'm making a final tour of the place I see Lori's sister Mickie waiting in the lobby. She's a bit distant—suspicious?—but I gave her a long hug. Lori returned then and of course our plan had to be given up—we stood around talking, as in the old days—I woke.

July, no date

I'm in my house when a couple of trucks arrive outside—night—and I go out and see who they are—they are workmen with orders to make certain state-required changes to my house. I study their papers—I think I had to sign them—and take them inside to go to work.

Family or friends sitting around in a living room unlike mine, laughing and smoking. I feel I have to go and check the work. The upstairs workman, who was supposedly adjusting a door to better fit its frame, has had the idea to remove all the plaster from the walls around and going up the stairs. I'm furious—demanding a reason—he remains calm, smiling and obtuse. I swear I won't pay for any of this. I find other things going wrong—I'm the only one noticing the insanity. They've taken out the wood-burning stove and installed a gigantic heater thing of enameled steel, taller than me.

I can't remember how or why I left the house to deal with all this, but next I was in a coffee shop being casually mocked or teased by other patrons (connected somehow to the workmen in my house). Bizarre things were happening to my seat or stool—rising and sinking—and some of the patrons knew it was being manipulated by powerful people in another location—just for the fun of it, apparently.

October, no date

Two remarkable dreams on two nights. The first I see now as connected to one of a few weeks back, which was another of those where I am unable to find my way to an important meeting through scenery that keeps changing, getting useless misdirection from nice or uncaring people. In this one I finally made clear to someone—a functionary in a huge hotel—that I have, in effect, a disability and am unable to find my way around or grasp geographical space. He tried to help but I ended up lost anyway. Then the next night, I was lost once again, trying to get to a lecture—the usual missteps, arrivals at unwanted places. Finally in a sort of department store where I encountered several girl children—blonde—obviously sisters. Then another, coming out via a dark staircase—their identical mother, carrying a baby. We began talking about children, seated now at a picnic table. It had grown dark. A man she said was her husband was there too—she insisted that he was dead, and he did look rather zombie-like and eroded. He kept making scary faces at me but I wasn't convinced. I was talking to the woman about these dreams I have where I get hopelessly lost trying to get to somewhere or go someplace—"And I suspect this is one," I said. She talked with me about this and tried to soothe my despairing exasperation—I really had had it. I can't remember anything she said to me, except that it was comforting. The talk turned to books. I woke up.

When I fell back into sleep again, I found myself still looking for that lecture, now ending up in an auditorium, but the wrong one—a dance performance underway—more like performance art—an artist performing his famous "Cosmic Fixations" piece, which consisted mostly of interacting with a steel door and an elevator door, seeming to draw steel rods out of the screw or bolt-holes of the doors with his fingers. When it was done he received a huge ovation, fans seeming to know just when it had come to an end and rushing the stage *en massse*, and me with them. The artist fled the stage via the steel door he had done his work on, with fans in pursuit, out into a large lobby. He resembled Peter Nigrini in his nonchalant air of expertise. Having heard that the lecture was still on, I asked if he knew where it was happening. He started giving me instruction but I told him it would be hopeless—"go left" would mean nothing after the first turns—and to him too I confessed my disability. He listened carefully, and what he said then was, "You should call the Red Cross Girls and ask one of them to be a guide." Immediately I saw the answer to my problem. "Or the Student Aid Society," I said, thinking that they volunteered to help visitors in just my difficulties. "Of course!" I woke up, delighted, my burden lifted.

November, no date

Dreaming falling off again and rarely up to earlier standards. One long and realistic one, a member of the series above, when I'd bought a car (I'd recently bought two, one for me, one for a daughter). In the dream I was trying out the car on a snowy hill—astonishing power and traction—but pushing it to the limit revealed weaknesses, and I had reason to return it. This became a quest dream, of course, as I tried to find the original mechanic who'd checked it out—driving through a dark town into the country—finding a place that was both it and not, a ramshackle spread under a mountain. Nice people, but they sent me off to someone else who would know where I was to go—lost my way *[realizing, when I later woke, that in dreams there are no actual ways to lose in a dream]*—stopped at another, similar place and was told Oh, yes, that place—I know where you mean—Mr. [name] knows where that is, go through the office there and ask him. I did find Mr. [name], a nice guy as everyone had been, and he sort of remembered the way, but he said that what I really had to do was to go to a house nearby where someone lived who would be able to tell me exactly—he started to explain how to get to *that* house, and I gave up in despair, weeping in frustration at how impossible it all was, how I'd never find the place, and how tired I was of being directed to such places by people who were just tormenting me and were anyway *completely imaginary!* At which I woke.

March 22, 2011

A lighter one—also with cars: Watching an early silent comedy about nuns, one a man in disguise, who's discovered by the other nuns and runs away, with the real nuns in pursuit. He climbs up a high wall and the pursuing nuns grab his feet to pull him down, but his legs simply extend as they pull, as in a cartoon. —Then another film, or an extension of that one, where the trick of the legs was explained—telescoping fake legs hidden under the habit he wore. Then I found myself either in the movie or beside a car that had appeared in the movie, a cartoonish open two-seater, and I got in and found I could make it go. I drove around in it, the ancient gears working with wonderful smoothness.

December 5

Dreams may be coming back after months of bits or nothing. Last night one in which I was standing in a crowd in a great hall—I can't remember why we were all crowded together—but someone whom I knew broke into the circle to tell me I had been chosen to be some sort of high Papal official—the great hall was part of the Vatican. I tried to resist—I knew this person, but not in a cassock, as now—and I tried to joke with him; he was to be my assistant, and was much taller than me, which I said would be ridiculous. Having none of this, he only hustled me through a vast gallery to an auditorium, where he showed me to a seat—an inconspicuous spot. (Maybe the announcement of my nomination was supposed to be a surprise.) I was thinking that I ought to find a way to get out of this, but maybe it would be fun, hanging around Rome. I wondered if it would be remunerative—I imagined showing the girls some rich gift I'd been given. I asked my assistant/keeper who anyway had voted on this position. Oh, he said, several bodies, including the Sacred Nuns. A huge crowd had now filled the auditorium, waiting. One woman tried to determine whether the audience spoke French, or English, or what other, by yelling out words for directions and listening for who answered back, or rather how many did. *Gauche!* she cried. *Derriere! Sinistra!*—I thought the girls would think that was funny. I was pondering my acceptance speech when I woke up.

May 29, 2012

Wish I could remember more of how it began—it was long—I was in the opening days of a romance with a man; we'd met in some seaside town where we were both staying, now sharing a hotel room, waking up together. He was young, fem but not swish, just nice. I did think I loved him, or at least that we were good together—tender, interested in each other. There was no sex—I thought we ought to shower first, brush teeth, but we only lay around on the bed talking. Looked out the windows at the beach below. He thought it was very sad that the weather wasn't beautiful (it looked all right to me), and I asked if little things like that often made him sad. Lay down beside him, kissed his cheek (no bristles!) and throat.

Then another somehow connected to that one—I had put on, or someone had put on me, an antique knight's helmet with a broad throat protector, and now I couldn't get it off. Someone (sort of like the boyfriend) was trying to extricate me, talking about an acetylene torch or a saw, and I was horrified—at last realized that the throat part could be safely pulled apart enough to get it off.

December 23

Months since I have had a dream about which I remember enough to write it down.

This one began with me in a borrowed apartment in a city unfamiliar to me, with some sort of meeting or class to go to. I prepared by choosing, from a limited wardrobe, a white jacket and a pair of white shorts. Decided to change. Put on a pair of khakis. Tried to organize the apartment—a mass of books and papers and spilled suitcases—then looked again at myself in the mirror, to find that the khakis were filthy, covered with ash from a fireplace and grease from food. Going to the unmade bed for something discarded but clean, I felt around in the covers—and found my cat. (I've had cats, but not in years.) She liked to get into the warmth under the covers, but I had worried that she couldn't breathe under there and would pass out and suffocate—and yes, though warm, she'd died—I pulled away the covers and found her still. She was a black-and-white cat I had decades ago. I felt terrible, and moreover had no idea what to do with her. The owner or landlord just then knocked on my door—he ran a summer writing program I was part of. The apartment was now an absolute mess—dropped or spilled piles of mostly comic books. I asked if he could help me to deal with the cat, and he said he would. To reward him, I took from my pocket a pill—a red and yellow capsule. (Somehow I knew he was into drugs.) He held out a hand for it, but as I put it there I dropped it and it rolled under the bed. I got down to find it, pushing it away from under a bureau, but when I went to stand up I stepped on it. I held up to him the little squashed thing and asked if he still wanted it. Woke.

After these many months of deep or silly or scary dreams that came, unfolded, and vanished away, I have mostly been unable to recover dreams, if in fact I have dreams at all. Following are a few additions from long after: 2014–2021.

2014, no date

I was involved with people in a tavern or restaurant, either working with them or boarding there—rackety working-class people. One woman resembled a person in my recent writing workshop who'd rejected my help (politely). She, or another, had a child, a toddler or even younger, a son. With no objections from the group, she'd put the baby aboard a long-distance bus, to be taken who knows where. When I understood this, I ran out to the bus—the baby was there in a carrier beside the driver, who had no thought but to get going.

I could see no solution but to go with the baby myself, raise it and care for it (I seemed in the dream to be young). I begged the driver to wait while I went to pack some things—confronted the people in the bar—told them this was terrible. Threw stuff in a small bag and rushed out, of course finding the streets changed and the bus nowhere to be found. Returned to the gang, who sympathized, remotely, and the talk turned to other matters, though I felt—as in previous dreams—a feeling of painful tenderness and love, and was sorry for the child.

March, no date

Very long one—began with my showing up for a psychotherapeutic appointment in a city. It was a huge establishment with many therapists. I was scheduled for a kind of hydrotherapy environment with a young male attendant. We went into a shower or wet room and I was standing in the water and so was he, and he was trying in some fashion to help me. Then I saw that the boy was actually a young woman. She said she had to take off her clothes in this room, and she was naked, afraid and embarrassed now but also fetching. I came close to her, very gently, but it was evident she was in great distress from our situation and our nakedness, so I left, or she did, and it was apparent that the session had ended. I went out and back to the huge waiting area, very troubled that my presence had done something wrong and harmed her emotionally or psychologically. I went to the desk and asked for an emergency appointment with my regular therapist, who was also the head of therapy here. I wanted to confess my behavior in the shower before the girl could lodge a complaint or have a breakdown. The person at the desk said, Oh no, you know he's Jewish and the Jewish holidays are this week—look here! And she showed me a calendar with all the dates taken. I didn't know what to do and loitered around the lobby explaining to myself how stupid I had been and thinking of the girl and wondering if I should just go back to the apartment I'd borrowed in Brooklyn.

Then somehow I was going to the therapist's *house*, a huge estate, and it turned out that he wasn't occupied with the holidays but dead, and on this day there was to be a big memorial service. In an open amphitheater there was to be a sort of cavalry tattoo, arranged in his honor. Everyone watching was touched but not mournful, and they cheered when one rider known to many of them rode out from the ranks blowing a silver trumpet. He wore a white uniform with a tall busby in white fur and a short cloak and seemed to be enjoying himself immensely. Woke up.

July 6, 2015

Without any introduction I am seated at a huge round table with many other people. Much talk I don't remember hearing. But it becomes clear that the table occupies a very large room with high wide windows, and I understand that it's a town meeting. The town manager introduces topics for discussion, addressing me particularly, but what's at issue is the town helicopter, which needs repair or replacement. I pretend to know that our small town had somehow acquired a helicopter—*oh yes, sure.*

    I lost the track of the meeting and went to the windows, from which i could see wide lawns and large trees, and people—townsfolk, I guessed—walking away from the building and going out through a line of hedges, seeming very small to me.

October 2021, no date

Far fewer memories of dreams in this year. I began to dream a kind of dream that was (or is) like streaming video: that is, I watch the events and sometimes hear the voices but am not a participant, only a witness. Many of these take place outdoors, or in woods or fields; most of the persons are children, or young people; often there's an older leader or guide I don't recognize but whom I seem to know anyway. Whatever they are doing in these groups vanishes away almost instantly when I wake.

October, no date

A dream that began (or opened on) myself and a friend—no one I knew in waking life—traveling in a pickup along a country road at night. We reached a farmhouse where we met a young woman, beautiful, a mass of tight blond curls. My friend from the truck knew her and knew she and I were—as he said—made for each other, and we were.

Later, I'd returned to my own house, knowing that she'd come there, and my friend came in after, smiling as though the getting-together of her and me was his doing. She was laughing and embraced me and her eyes sparkled with happy tears (only in dreams does this happen, I think), and I woke up in happy tears myself.

Possibly November, no date

Driving in a pickup with a young man (not the man in the previous truck, and both of us younger) to a sort of building site or storage sheds, the landscape flat and dusty but sunlit. When we arrived at the complex—all the buildings were of raw boards with metal roofs—we saw a number of adolescent boys without much to do. They took turns standing on a narrow walkway or wooden bridge over a stable yard where a couple of horses stood. The boys were teasing one another, daring others to jump off the bridge down into the horse pound. The driver of the truck I was in—like the boys, shirtless, blond, but older—told them not to be stupid and get back to work.

Then he drove away with me out of the compound and down a straight, flat dirt road that ran across a dusty treeless field. We drove past a house made of bare boards but tall and with many windows. "I remember that place," I said, picturing an old farm woman I'd seen. "I washed those windows for her once." Woke up laughing.

No date

I was sick in bed in a dark room. My wife came in to see me. She looked nothing like my actual wife, though I didn't really notice this in the moment. She looked, in fact, like Betty Boop: tangled mass of black hair, stark white oval face, little red lips. Her eyes were huge, with white pupils and black lenses, wide open. She bent her face to me and kissed me, the eyes coming near my face. Wonderful.

December 14

Don't remember anything of the beginning—faint notion, when awake, of moving with a lot of people on the move, coming to a large, ancient stone building or compound. I found myself ascending a spiral stone walk or ramp—arching stone ceiling, tiny windows or none. I remember no thoughts of this, or why I was alone—but at some point, I saw, down where I had begun climbing, a cop in full uniform. He came up to where I was as I went down, and we met. I asked where I was, etc. He was pleasant but not helpful. He mentioned his gun, in a holster. Must be expensive, I said. Oh yes, but his was officially supplied to him. More chat with this personable small man—on waking I can't match him to any actual person I know or know of, though it was clear that he was a guide, or bore a welcome to this place; and I knew, when I woke, where I had been.

Afterword

I have recorded no further dreams; most of what I dream now are the movielike ones, where I watch people I mostly don't know, whose voices I can rarely hear or understand: mostly large numbers, many of them outdoors, in woods or fields or open city spaces, mostly children and a few adults watching over them.

In one of these dreams it was night, cold; the setting was Washington, D.C., but not in this year—it seemed to be the early 1960s. A government worker, a young, blond woman, signals a cab; as she gets in, she sees another government official, male, known to her, walking alone; she signals to him to join her. He does, gratefully; a cool, self-assured tall man, good-looking; they chat lightly, and she says she's going to join some others at an apartment nearby, nice people, smart—would he like to come? He does—anyway I next experience him there, standing a bit aloof, not removing his beautiful overcoat, accepting a drink—others on couches gossiping. Eventually (whatever that can mean) he goes with her in another cab to drop her at her own apartment building; she's tired and cold and leans against his shoulder. At her place she casually invites him up, and in the apartment he observes the pictures and objects, flowers in vases, open books lying on other open books, all reflecting her. Nothing seems to happen but might later on. The last I see of him, he's in his own place, smaller than hers, and dim. He reads the paper. There's a cat.

That's all. Everything that had seemed to happen was at once happening in the world of John Kennedy and also not in that world, but in this one. The tall man in the fine overcoat, his cool warmth, was not me. In the following months, nothing like it appeared in dreamspace—and now may not ever.

John Crowley lives with his wife in the hills above the Connecticut River in northern Massachusetts. He is the father of twins and the author of over a dozen novels.